CHA CHAS in LONDON

WRITTEN BY

Corky Ballas &
Carolina Orlovsky

ILLUSTRATED BY

David Estrada

PREFACE

Chloe and her brother George are from Toronto, Canada. George, being older than his sister Chloe, had met Mr. Spin several times while he was teaching lessons and workshops.

George at 12 had developed a passion for dance and begged his parents to allow him to train with Mr. and Mrs. Spin in London.

Chloe being 10, two years younger and also an aspiring dancer, wanted to follow her brother and dance with Mr. and Mrs. Spin's son, Alexander Spin.

George and Chloe's parents were worried, but after several meetings with World Champion dancers Mr. and Mrs. Spin, they agreed to let Chloe move to London to train for dance and attend school.

Hi! I'm Nosey the "studio" dog!

A black taxi moved fast

down the crowded streets of London.

Chloe's heart was beating so loud and she could feel

butterflies dancing

in

her

tummy.

Chloe's taxi pulled up

to a dark, old
brick building with a muddy,
green door.

"All right, we are here," said the driver cheerfully.
"This is it?" asked Chloe. "I thought it would be more glamorous."
Chloe took a long, deep breath
and stepped out of the car.
Her legs were trembling.

3

As Chloe walked inside, she was immediately greeted by a staircase and a sign that read:

Dance Studio Suite 602.

She dragged her bags up SIX flights of stairs, which led to the most narrow hallway she had ever seen.

When she finally found the studio, she tried to peek in through the frosted glass. She couldn't see anything but she could hear the sounds of Cha Cha music

dancing through the air.

She pushed the door open.

It was freezing in the room but everyone was sweaty.

There were couples dancing and it felt like they were

m o v i n g at the speed of light! Chloe's brother,

George, spotted her and ran to give her

a hug as she

leaped into his arms.

"Come with me,"

said George, "I want you to meet everyone. This is Alex Spin, he will be your partner, and these are his parents, Mr. and Mrs. Spin." They all smiled, greeting her with a hug and a kiss on each cheek. They seemed rather

fancy.

Mrs. Spin told Chloe to change into her practice clothes, get her shoes on, and warm up. Her lesson with Mr. Spin and Alex would be starting in exactly 7 minutes. Judging by the tone of her voice, Chloe knew

she meant
business.

"Okay Chloe, show me your basic,"
said Mr. Spin.

Chloe took a deep breath

and did her best Cha Cha for him.

As Alex danced the ten Cha Cha steps,

   Chloe realized that he was so much better and faster than she was. All of a sudden her cheeks turned a

   hot red and she ran off crying, feeling that

she had

disappointed

everyone.

She burst into the girls dressing room,

sobbing over her awful Cha Cha.

How was she ever going to get this?

Everyone here was so

much

better than her.

She wished she could call her mom.

She always knew what to do.

George knocked on the door and asked to come in. Chloe wiped her tears away and looked around to make sure no one else was there.

"Okay, come in," she whimpered.

"Chloe, what are you doing?" he asked. "How could you come all this way and even think of giving up? Sure, today it's hard but guess what? It was hard for me, too, in the beginning. But tomorrow it will get easier, and the day after that easier still, and before you know it,

you will be dancing."

She wiped away her tears and asked, "You think so?"

"I know so," said George.

"It's okay to make mistakes, but it's not okay to quit. You just gave up and giving up is not an option, Chloe. Not here, not anywhere, and especially not with Mr. and Mrs. Spin. They are World Champions. Mr. Spin does not let anybody use the word CAN'T."

"All right, I am ready and this time no matter what, no matter how many mistakes I make, I will keep at it," said Chloe.

"I can do this!"

"That's the spirit, Chloe!" exclaimed George. Although there were no fancy ballrooms, sparkly costumes, or diamond tiaras, she marched out with her head held high and said, "Let's Cha Cha, Mr. Spin." With enough hard work, Chloe knew that it would all be possible one day!

"We have a lot of work to do," said Mr. Spin.

"Let's start from the very beginning."

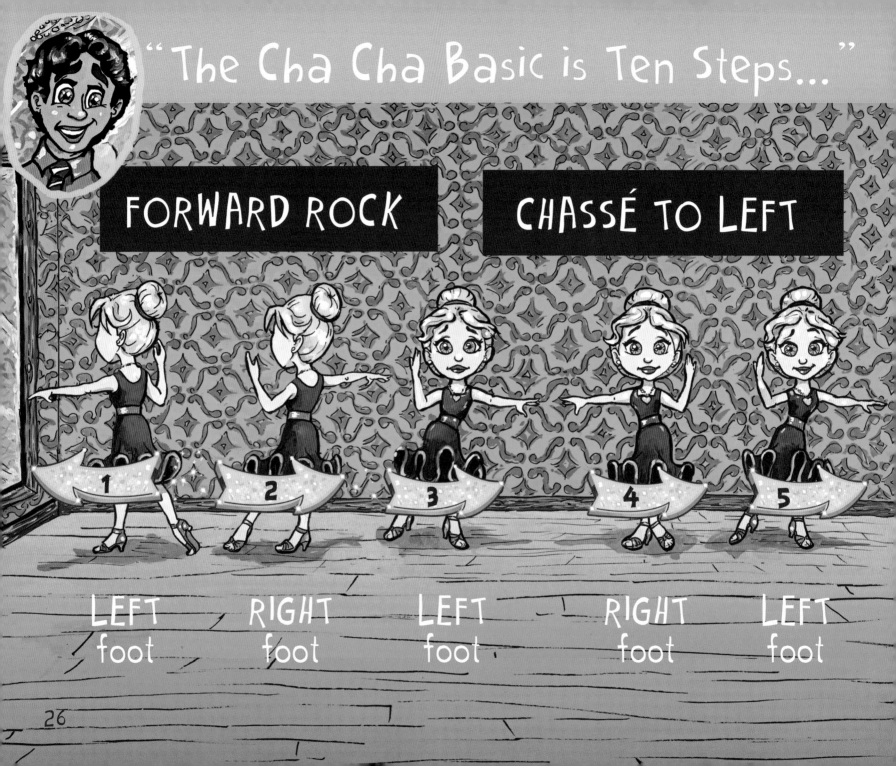

BACK ROCK

CHASSÉ TO RIGHT

RIGHT foot

LEFT foot

RIGHT foot

LEFT foot

RIGHT foot

After her lesson with Mr. Spin, Chloe practiced the steps he had taught her. She practiced...

over...

...and over...

...and over...

...and over...

...and over...

...and over...

...and over...

...and over...

...and over...

After a lot of hard work and practicing, she felt proud and excited that she could dance the Cha cha to the speed of the music without any mistakes. She was ready to show Mr. Spin her progress!

29

As she danced the Cha Cha for Mr. Spin, she felt more confident in her steps. She knew it wasn't perfect but felt proud of herself for trying so hard. Chloe was excited to keep practicing and get better and better.

The End

Now it's YOUR turn to learn the dance...

To learn to dance for free visit
ChloeBook.com

Lesson LEFT FOOT ROCK STEP

Step <u>forward</u> with your LEFT foot.

Step <u>back</u> with your RIGHT foot.

Lesson CHASSÉ TO THE LEFT

Step <u>side</u> with your LEFT foot. Close your feet. Step <u>side</u> with your LEFT foot.

Lesson RIGHT FOOT ROCK STEP

Step <u>back</u> with your RIGHT foot.

Step <u>forward</u> with your LEFT foot.

Lesson CHASSÉ TO THE RIGHT

Step <u>side</u> with your RIGHT foot. Close your feet. Step <u>side</u> with your RIGHT foot.

I would like to dedicate this book to my daughter Lea; every time we part, my heart aches. She inspires me every day and I am so grateful to be her mom. May her dreams have no boundaries.

I would also like to thank my parents who did the most difficult thing any parent could do - they let me go. If it was not for their love, trust, and support, I would have never had the courage to move to New York City at 18 to follow my dreams of becoming a professional dancer. They could never know how truly homesick I was for them and Toronto. It was their love and belief in me that got me through the most difficult times.

May this book offer a light to anyone who wants to live a dream and the true reality of the sacrifices it takes, because it takes a village of teachers, friends, mentors, and family to help you along your path and never, ever let you give up. So keep dreaming and letting your heart guide your feet.

CAROLINA ORLOVSKY, Co-Author

This story is dedicated to my son Mark Ballas and my experience raising and training Derek and Julianne Hough, who lived with us for several years in London, England. Many of you have seen all of us on the famous hit show *Dancing with the Stars*. They learned how important work ethic, discipline, and setting goals is in life, and look at them now! :) My wish is that all children will be inspired to adopt these important life skills in everything they do.

What I know for sure is...

"Anyone Can Learn To Dance with an Open Mind."

CORKY BALLAS, Co-Author

FUTURE BOOKS COMING SOON!